CU01019820

HERMIONE

After her mother's death,
Hermione looks after her father,
only to witness his decline.
Finally summoning the strength
to live her own life, she
leaves, and starting with a
long train ride to London she
begins her journey of
self-discovery.

Also by Daniel Tribe

FULL MOON RED SUN

Daniel Tribe

HERMIONE

EverGreen Graphics

CRAIGWEIL ON SEA
ALDWICK

Daniel Tribe

HERMIONE

First published in the United Kingdom 2001 by
EverGreen Graphics

This edition first published in 2002

Printed and bound in the United Kingdom by
Creative Print & Design Group
(Book Division)
Blaenau, Gwent, Wales NP23 5XW

ISBN 1-900192-04-7

Design and Production by Cecil Smith
Typeset in Joanna MT by
EverGreen Graphics
11 The Drive, Craigweil On Sea, Aldwick,
West Sussex PO21 4DU

MEMBERS OF THE GUILD OF MASTER CRAFTSMEN

HERMIONE

Chapter

1

A S SHE LOOKED OUT OF THE RAIN SMUDGED WINDOW OF the second class rail carriage, only the leaves on the trees let her know that it was summer. The sky was mottled grey, it was the middle of the afternoon but it felt like dusk. In a sense her whole life had been like this journey, she had sat quietly as other people got on and off, as if indifferent to her, that she was simply part of their landscape.

Now though it would be different, she had met Philip. At first nothing seemed particularly remarkable about him, perhaps the way he spoke, in that he was from the south, and it reminded her of when she was a child, before they had moved north. He had slowly become more precious to her, until they became lovers, and now she was finally leaving to be with him.

She had seldom been comfortable, either at home or school. Her father, a rudely handsome man whose dark hair and brown eyes she had inherited, seemed to change after the move. They had gone to the north because of his job, but his early gentleness towards her disappeared there, and her mother became quiet and introverted. School had carried on more or less as it had started.

'You're a bit posh aren't you!' said Sheila Wilson on her first day. 'We'll soon learn ya!', and they did. Their toughness was reflected in the stones and bricks of the Victorian factories that had endured and stood looking down on them, as they made their way in the freezing rain through the school gates, to submit to the monotony of yet another day. Beneath the stone exterior though was real warmth. Sheila was in fact a kindly soul, battered by the elements, her surroundings, where 'You look out for yourself, no one else will,' but Hermione struggled, even under Sheila's tutelage.

The train had stopped at Preston and women and young children were clambering into her carriage followed by older ones travelling noisily in gangs of two or three. An elderly couple came and sat in the empty seat opposite her and the woman smiled at Hermione.

'Where do you want me to put this?' the husband said, struggling with the small but overweight piece of hand luggage.

'Down there love, just under the table. I'm sure this young lady won't mind, will you?' she smiled, looking again at Hermione.

'No, that's fine' she replied and the husband dutifully stooped to put the bag firmly on the floor between them.

After the move north her mother didn't make new friends and there were not many visitors. Yet nearly everyone in their street was kind, and Hermione got to know them as she ran to get sweets at the corner shop; blackjacks, fruit salads and sherbet fountains. The summers were hot, butterflies swarmed around the white and purple buddleia that hung like magic lanterns above the black railings on top of their garden wall. She used to try and count the Red Admirals and Tortoiseshells as they lay basking in the sun. Before he began to change, her father sometimes came back from work early to cut the grass on the back lawn, and she would take him a glass of lemonade when he had finished. He'd take it between his big red hands and finish it all in one large gulp, and she watched the droplets spill onto his chin as he finished it off and handed her back the glass to take into the kitchen. In the corner of the garden there was a swing, and he used to stop cutting the grass and push her higher and higher until she shrieked for him to stop. Then, over a period of time, he didn't come home early to cut the grass anymore, he stopped playing with her and the evenings before bed were spent alone with her mother, whom she loved dearly.

When the buddleia had stopped flowering and the leaves on the trees began to turn, winter descended in its fullness over the house like a dark cloak which engulfed them. Sometimes she heard her father come in long after she had gone to bed, he shouted at her mother, his voice penetrating the thick joists and floorboards of their Victorian house.

'So what if I do like a drink after work. You should get out more yourself, moping round the house all day, it's bad for you'.

Three years later her mother died. Hermione thought it was of a broken heart, the doctor had said cancer. Her father, drinking heavily by then, became crippled with remorse. He drank more, and the once handsome face became puffy and red.

'You're all I've got lass, you'll never leave me will you?' he would say if he decided to spend the evening in, drinking at home in front of the T.V., and Hermione stayed and cared for him for eight years after her mother's death. She got a job, a sales assistant in a bookshop. She spent the evenings reading when he was at the pub, sometimes she went out with the girls from the shop to the local cinema, but she felt generally detached from life. The shock of her mother's death passed slowly for her. Every Sunday she went to tend the grave alone, he simply couldn't bring himself to go. She tried to comfort him, but he became worse.

She felt partially numb, living quietly with her thoughts, her memories of childhood and her books. She educated herself, her reading went in stages and she tended to have a blitz on something before moving on, twentieth century novels, painting, and more recently history. Once she arrived at the 1930's it all slowed down for her, as if she got stuck there, in a world of pre-war elegance, of art deco and Bellinis.

Philip gave her life. It happened slowly, and she emerged from her cocoon. She didn't tell her father, he would have been difficult. They met secretly, an afternoon off walking in the park, an evening at the cinema, meals out. Philip worked for a publishing company and she had met him in the bookshop. She noticed his voice, rather the way he pronounced his words, and as she looked up he had caught her eye and smiled. The next day he came back in, and the day after that he asked her to go out for a drink with him.

'I don't drink' she blurted.

'What? Not even a cup of tea!' he smiled, and she warmed to him.

Their first kiss was under a sycamore tree in the park in autumn. She was laughing and he pulled her towards him, and suddenly his mouth was touching hers, his lips pressing hers apart allowing him to explore her taste, her warmth. They made love for the first time a week later in his room in the hotel where he was staying. He was gentle, she had grown more familiar with his kisses, and the anticipation excited her.

During the winter that followed, her father spent more evenings at home. Hermione would come straight in from the bookshop, set and light the coal fire in the front room, pause to watch the smoke curl beneath the polished copper hood before it snaked back up the chimney. Her mother loved the fire, its dark green Victorian tiles and elegant mantelpiece, a testimony of better times. 'It's like our fireplace used to be at home' she would say as they spent the long evenings together. The house had been bought with the remains of her inheritance, and she tended it and the garden with loving care until her death.

After Hermione had set and lit the fire, she would prepare her father's supper and begin cleaning and doing the washing and ironing. He kept beer and whisky in a pantry off the kitchen, it had a small window which they always left open so that the beer was cool even in the summer. Her father would get back home at any time between half past six and half past nine, and depending on the time he would have had between two and six pints before coming in through the back door. If it was late, he started on the whisky straightaway, and she tried to avoid him. She would put his supper in front of him on the kitchen table, and he would complain about the food or that the plate had a small chip in it, a serviette was stained, there was only a paper napkin instead of a cotton one.

'I don't want this, it's ruined, get me some bread and cheese or something, I'll have me supper in front of the fire'.

If she could manage to get away, after settling him down in the chair onto which her mother gazed down from a photograph on the mantelpiece, she would escape to her room, to a book. Hours later when it was safe she would come down and put the fireguard in front of the burning embers, pick up his plate and the whisky and lock the back door before going back to her room.

When Philip was in town they met when they could, in the lunch hour, her afternoon off in the week and occasionally on Saturdays, if she could get one of the other girls to cover for her in the shop. Apart from their lovemaking, Philip was kind and interested in her. He didn't speak a great deal about himself, or the details of his own life other than his work at the publishing company which he liked. Their warehouse and printers in Blackburn gave him the opportunity to see her, and he brightened the darkness of the winter of her life.

She looked out of the window again, down onto the huge expanse of a redbrick aqueduct and the river which tumbled between its piers that straddled the banks either side and beyond to the outskirts of the town, to the chimney stacks which glowed like extinct volcanoes, having once given life to the fertile plains below. The mills had closed long ago, one or two still gleaned a living as recycling yards where huge bales of discarded clothing were graded into piles or broken back down into fibre to be re-woven or sold in Pakistan and West Africa. Others still lay empty, refusing change. Like the aqueduct, they had formed part of a struggle which now seemed long forgotten but to which they bore witness. They reminded her of the factories near the school and the pact she had made with Sheila Wilson never to end up working there. Where was Sheila now? She had last bumped into her pushing a pram in the rain with another small child clinging on to it.

'I've got another one on the way', she said, 'I've told him, he'll have to get the snip – can't be doing with all this!' The rain poured down her face onto her shiny mac, Sheila was resilient as ever. 'Are you seeing anyone then?' she asked knowingly. 'I've heard these rumours, you know! I've heard he's dead good looking!'

Hermione blushed but was grateful that Sheila wouldn't notice as the rain splattered her face too, 'Well, he's a friend really but I like him and he takes me out' she said sheepishly.

'You should leave him at 'ome love! That's what I do with my fella, and go out with the lasses. You know we go to the Bull or up the Star sometimes … eh' they've got a male stripper up there Friday nights with a great big willy like a chuffin' donkey, you should come up it's a right laugh!'

'Oh, I've still got my dad, you know …'

'Ah, time that old bastard moved on isn't it, the trouble he gave you, and your mum. Any road, I'd best be on my way, it's time for this lot's tea and they'll soon start bloody screaming!' Sheila smiled and turned walking off in the rain, 'C'mon Tracey, mummy's going this way', and Tracey splashed along beside the pram.

She gazed out over the cooling towers south of Warrington Bank East station, they dominated the landscape for miles around. Were these the mothers of that warmth of spirit? She had once brought Sheila Wilson home, and her father growled from upstairs 'Who's that? Who's there? Tell 'em to go away!'

'It's alright Dad, it's just a friend from school', but Hermione was overcome with embarrassment, and she never took anyone home again.

Now, leaving, she wondered if all that she had heard of southerners was true.

'The difference between us and them is that up 'ere everyone is really friendly, and people say what they mean. Down there they're different, I've 'eard that a lot of neighbours don't even know each other!' It was Mrs Moore, who had taken Hermione into her bosom from the first day she saw her, running back from the sweet shop. 'My, you're in a hurry aren't you! You've just moved in 'aven't you, up road? Now, next time you're passing you pop in here, I've got some special toffee apples I cook for my grand-children!' Hermione did, and she had long since lost count of the hours amounting to days that she spent with Mrs Moore, telling her about everything, as Mrs Moore had a knack of winkling it out. She was never specific about her father, but Mrs Moore knew, and she was always kindly towards her mother if she saw her.

'I've known that Sheila Wilson since she was just a wee one, bonnie wee thing, you don't want to take too much notice of her!' she said when Sheila had been teasing Hermione. 'Changeable as the weather that one, but she'll settle down one day, you see.'

The cooling towers were left far behind and she

gazed out onto maize fields and small farms dotted around the hillside. She thought of her father again, a man driven to a working life he could barely stand, so far away from his dream. He sometimes talked about an idea that beneath the 'normal world' as he put it, was another world which we never touch. He called it 'they'. 'They won't let you, you won't be able to do that, you'll never get away with it, it's not just the government but those that's interested in power, in control. That's what I mean by 'they' lass?'

She looked at the seagulls following a blue tractor on a stark brown field as it furrowed north and south with pleasing inevitability. People moved like puppets along the edge of a canal by some barges, bright green and yellow, dull brown and aubergine. Had she inherited more than the darkness of her father's hair and eyes? He had been a thinker, but shut his thoughts off because they were too painful. It was this, this sensitivity that her mother had loved so much and when it went it was as if her love went with it too.

At Crewe they passed a sign 'Blackpool Pleasure Beach', where bears on a roller coaster said 'Where Will Your Journey End?' The sidings were full of old trains, with names like 'St Roland Hill' or 'Peter Howarth CBE'. A blonde woman on a poster told her it was 'Tango Time', and next to it a bearded face carved in stone stared out at her from an arch. The old couple opposite got off and for the time being nobody replaced them. She stretched her legs as the train pulled out of the station, and once again looked at the world through glass. Against the darkness of the trees that lined the bank, it acted as a mirror, she could see herself passing like a ghost in front of it. One moment she could see herself clearly, the colour of her blouse, her skin, sun glasses, and then she was gone, replaced by a field of stubble or maize. She looked out onto a man-made lake where a solitary cormorant gazed into the water. The bank rose higher, a brutal end to the gardens that backed onto it, then it suddenly dipped to reveal green fields where horses grazed peacefully. There was a quarry in the distance, overlooked by a redbrick Victorian farmhouse. A white horse stood alone by another small lake, cows grazed nearby and then they too were gone, far in the distance. She was passing through lush countryside, willow trees overhung the dark blue waters of streams which snaked peacefully across the ripening fields of corn. A kestrel hovered outside the window and she felt she could reach out and touch it, it was so close. A boy in a striped jumper stood on the corner of a small road; in the field next to him sheep nibbled at the grass, oblivious to the passing carriages. The sky had cleared, lighting up the shadows beneath the trees, planes, oaks, sycamore and pines nestling in the gentle slopes of the countryside. If only they had moved here instead of town, perhaps things would have been better.

It was past four in the afternoon, she would now be getting ready to leave the shop to get back and prepare her father's tea. It was summer, and he would probably stay late in the pub. Sometimes he ate there, leaving the food she had prepared for him. What would he do when he went back tonight to an empty house and an empty table? At first he would curse, shout out for her. She had tried it once, staying quietly in her room instead of being in the kitchen for him when he came back. She could hear him stumbling around, barging into things, shouting out 'Where the bleeding 'ell are ya?' He'd do the same tonight, only this time he'd go back and look for her before getting out the whisky and drinking himself into oblivion.

Near Rugby she gazed out onto a distant church spire, small holdings, and old farm buildings where some horses stood on the crest of a hill looking down over a new housing estate. Clouds were darkening, closing in. She noticed a sign saying it was 102 miles to London. There she would have to cross the city and change trains to her final destination, to Philip. In the distance on the horizon a pine forest was silhouetted against the sky but it was dwarfed by four cooling towers, a solitary redbrick chimney and what looked like a colliery close to the railway line. Between them the church steeple glistened, but she felt that God had long ago abandoned the inhabitants of the town. The weather was changing noticeably, becoming distinctly bleak, the small roads leading away from the railway line glistened like serpents snaking their way through the dim grey light. There was no shadow to tell whether it was morning or evening, whether it was the beginning or the end. In the distance the rain had become so heavy over the hills that cars had put on their headlights, and they shone like alien eyes across the barren fields. Smoke from dying bonfires spread like a shroud across the face of the earth, as if to extinguish all at once its pulse, its heart beat.

A single lady who was about sixty five years old, had taken the seat opposite her. She wore an orange and green floral dress, an old gold watch, a mother of pearl brooch at her neck, a brown hat, brown shoes and a cream handbag. She looked tired, wore no make-up and soon after sitting down closed her eyes and began to drift into an uneasy sleep. She sat with her arms folded, moving her fingers as her eyelids flickered. There was no wedding ring on her finger, there were no rings at all. In the reflection of the glass her faced looked older, and she slept as if in death, still and pale. Surely when this woman was young, as young as Hermione was now, it would have been

Hermione

strange for her not to have found someone and married. She was not unattractive, even now, and in her youth she must have been fair, even good looking. Why then no ring? She had a copy of the Readers Digest beneath her handbag on her lap and the shoes, on reflection, were perhaps those of a schoolmistress, sturdy and solid. A spinster then? Her curiosity began to border on nosiness and Hermione didn't like herself for it. She turned again to gaze out of the window, away from the woman in case she woke, caught her eye and began talking.

The journey was ending as it had begun, beneath mottled grey skies and rain splattered windows. Euston loomed like a foreign shore in the sea of fog and rain that surrounded it, not a soul stirred beneath the dim blue and orange lights that lit their way as they passed the industrial sheds and small power plants around the station.

She crossed the city and it was only a short journey of about an hour before she reached her final destination, where Philip would be waiting. She thought of the time that she had last seen him. She waved goodbye as his train left Blackburn; a journey she thought she herself would never undertake. Now that she had, there could be no turning back.

Chapter

2

SHE HAD ARRANGED TO MEET HIM BY THE ENTRANCE OF the small country station. There was nowhere to sit, and she stood outside with her suitcase looking around the car park for his reassuring smile, for the comfort of his arms around her. She checked her watch, she was on time but thought he was probably late because of a delay at work or the traffic, and she leaned back slightly against the wall beneath the eaves of the station to shelter against the rain. Taxis and cars pulled up to collect other passengers, and eventually she was alone. More cars arrived, this time dropping people off, and she moved back inside the entrance for the additional shelter it offered. Half an hour passed, and she walked outside to cross the car park and telephone from one of the kiosks opposite. It was too late to phone his office, and there was no reply from home, so she went back to the station and waited.

The rain was incessant. There was a pub beyond the car park and the warm glow of its lights looked inviting, but if he turned up now and she wasn't there, no, it was better to wait. She bought a hot chocolate from the vending machine, it was sickly and sweet, she drank half and threw the rest away. Another London train arrived, but this time fewer passengers got off. It was the middle of the evening, they shuffled into waiting cars or taxis and soon she was alone again, tired and wet. She decided to cross the road to the pub. On the way she tried the phone again, there was still no reply, but he knew the station and would surely guess that if he was really late she would have gone to the pub to wait there.

Inside it was crowded and smoky, it smelt of stale beer, of her father. She wondered why anybody would go and drink in a place like that, dowdy and uninspiring. There was a pool table in the corner which was busy, everyone else, all men, were sitting at bar stools with half empty pints of lager in front of them, in the haze of cigarette smoke. She ordered an orange juice and sat on an old settle by a window with a clear view of the station entrance and the car park. The sky had darkened and the rain stabbed at the small windowpanes. She sat and waited.

After a second orange juice she picked up her case and braced herself to go back out, into the rain that fell like cold steel. The wind snatched the door from her hand as she opened it. The ticket clerk was near the station entrance, but no one had asked for her, it was dusk and soon night would fall. In desperation she went to the telephone kiosks and tried his home number again. The rain fell onto her neck as she opened the door, and the phone rang and rang. Opposite a taxi dropped off a young couple who ran laughing into the station and on the spur of the moment Hermione dashed across the car park before the taxi had time to pull off. She asked the driver to take her to a reasonable guesthouse and with a heavy heart she sat in the back seat, wishing, hoping and praying.

The guesthouse was a cliché of flock wallpaper, a pink candlewick bedspread and nosy landlady. She had a bath, went to bed and tried to sleep. She what if'd every possibility, but in her heart a new heaviness began to find a place and it sank her like a stone. She clutched at the willing suspension of disbelief, that there was an explanation and she was simply unable to put her finger on it, but the stone pulled her down into the dark waters of fear and loneliness, to the echoes of her father's voice 'You're bloody daft! I could have told you!', to the madness of hope, of a knock at the door saying there was a phone call for her, and she would hear Philip's voice.

She must have slept; the fingers of daylight prodded her awake. She washed and dressed and went straight to the pay phone in the hall. It was still too early to phone the office but she tried his home number and let it ring. There was still no reply. Succumbing to her worst fears, she telephoned the police and asked if there had been any serious accidents in the area involving Philip. They were helpful, but said they didn't need to run a check because fortunately there hadn't been anything within the last twenty-four hours. Perhaps he was at home, there was a fault on the line, the caller could hear it ringing but it didn't sound the other end. She would go to his house, and he would be in, wondering why she hadn't called.

The landlady called a local cab firm for her and it was only a fifteen minute ride to his house. It was more or less as she had imagined it, a solid cottage style in a quiet tree-lined road. He had told her about it, how he had converted the attic, restored a fireplace which had been covered up, taken down some of the internal walls to make it feel bigger.

She walked up the narrow garden path bordered by shrubs, noticing a small brightly coloured ball in the shadow of a leylandii tree in the corner. Some logs were stacked next to the front porch under the cover of the eaves of the house. Three bottles of milk were inside the porch, on top was a rain-smudged note that she couldn't read. She pressed the bell. There was no answer, and she pressed it again. This time she heard footsteps, which sounded as if they were coming down the stairs. Her heart missed a beat.

She could hear the safety chain being taken off, the click of the snib as the door opened. Behind it was a child, a boy, about twelve years old in school uniform. He smiled at Hermione, and said hello before turning and shouting up the stairs 'Mum! Mum, there's a lady here at the door', and then he disappeared. 'Mum' eventually came to the door in a dressing gown, her tangled long blonde hair unable to conceal her fine looks.

'Hello' said Hermione. 'I've come to see Philip Saunders, is he in?'

The blonde woman smiled. 'No. He's been away on a course at work for a couple of days. Can I help, I'm his wife?'

The words paralysed her, blood rushed around her body driven by a crazy heart, but to the outside world she stood motionless. The woman may have spoken again, if she did, Hermione didn't hear. She turned away and began walking. She was soaked by the rain, scenes of her life with Philip appeared in her mind, she made sense of some of them, the silences, changes of subject, but it was too late, she had been his fool. She found shelter at a bus stop, the wet seeped through her coat and dress, the silence echoed her angry solitude.

A green and cream bus arrived and she mechanically got up and onto the rear platform, conscious of the sickening smell of diesel. She bought a ticket for the train station and sat alone on one of the long seats at the back. She had walked in a circle, and the station was only two stops away. It was still raining as she made her way across the car park to the entrance and the ticket clerk. Two or three passengers had formed a small queue, she waited then turned round and went back to the taxi rank, to the guesthouse.

'My, you look like a drowned rat!' said the landlady, 'you can have the same room back again if you like, I've just had a cancellation, you're in luck.'

Hermione stayed there for three days, it could have been three weeks. She didn't eat but she did drink tea which she was able to make herself in the room. On the fourth day she went out, the weather had cleared and a watery sun lit the guesthouse lawn and trees around it. She walked into the town, just ten minutes away, and found a resting-place in 'Enrico's Café' where she bought a cheese sandwich and a cup of coffee. Enrico, or whatever his name was, was fat, dark and bald with a large moustache and a big smile. He was the ubiquitous Latin émigré, and he smiled as she paid him.

'Now we gotta put up with this weather! It's worse than the winter!'

'No, Enrico. You can tell it's summer, the rain's warmer!'

The cold steely tone of the voice made her heart skip a beat. It was like Philip's, clear and distinct, but it had an air of conscious superiority which thankfully Philip's had lacked. The speaker sat reading in a corner seat by the window.

'Good! I feel much better for that then!' quipped Enrico.

Hermione left half the sandwich, but drank the coffee. She would wreak revenge upon him, wreck his life as he had wrecked hers. She would go and see his wife, tell her everything, tell her the details of their times together, of their lovemaking. She would devote the rest of her life to her father, rescuing him from his drunkenness, from his despair which at times must have been so like the hell she now inhabited. She would go back. But this was a moment of comparative lucidity, and for the most part she remained in the dark, alone, with no-one to hear her cry.

'You want some more coffee?' Enrico smiled as he cleared the half-eaten sandwich and empty cup.

'Yes, yes please, thank you.' She could not go back. She had decided, she didn't know when, she would accept her fate. Her revenge would be that of silence. He would never know whether there would be a phone call, a letter quietly dropped, almost innocently, to lay on the carpet behind the front door, picked up perhaps by the innocent hands of a child and delivered open-eyed to his mother. But there would never be such a letter, Hermione could never harm a woman who was herself innocent, a victim. And the child, it was none of his doing either. It was better left, she would find a way to mend herself, she would struggle and find a way. She would never turn back.

So she sat and sipped her coffee. She had not expected to be supported financially by Philip, and had managed to save a small amount of money from her job in the book-store. It was enough to get by on for a few weeks, may be a month or so until she was able to find a job. She couldn't stay here, in a town where she might see him again. Almost anywhere would do, she reflected. She had seen plenty of countryside on her rail journey, she would go back to the station and take another train and go on, not for long, just long enough to get away from him.

Chapter

3

THE HUGE FARM MACHINE CRAWLED ACROSS THE EARTH like a giant insect, devouring and spitting out everything in its path. In the deep ochre light of the summer evening sun, it toiled alone. Most of the villagers sat by their hearths after supper, or meandered slowly with their dogs and children along to the river and the shade it offered beneath the planes and willows along its banks.

A month had passed since she had arrived in the small country town that nestled beneath the Downs. The unseasonal storms of the preceding month, the rain that had stabbed and slashed at her gave way to the sun that rose up over the hills and scattered the clouds, claiming its rightful place in the summer sky. She had found a room in a large Victorian country house that had been split into apartments and bed-sits. Bodding Dean Hall stood alone on high ground with extensive gardens laid to lawn. At their edge were walls of local stone, and behind them was a jungle of desolate gardens, long forgotten, leading down to the banks of the river. She seldom saw any of the other occupants and she often felt that she was there alone. Her money all but gone, she had found a job in the local library through the newspaper.

Compared to Bodding Dean Hall, the library was a warm and friendly building, built in the 16th century, timber-framed with leaded light windows and wide polished oak floorboards. She earned enough to pay the rent on her bedsit, with a modest amount left over for food. She had written to Mrs Moore, giving her the poste restante address. Philip had met Mrs Moore, he could be very persuasive and she didn't want him to track her down. She then arr-anged with the woman in the Post Office, by telling her she was avoiding a man, to get mail delivered to Bodding Dean, and the mail van went up there any-way. And so her untraceability in this respect was reasonable. She guessed that Mrs Moore would look in on her father from time to time, inevitably, no doubt, to be told that he didn't need her 'interfering', but Hermione knew it would take more than her father's drunkenness to frighten such a woman.

Life was slowly beginning to acquire a pattern for her. The aching fear in her stomach ceased when she was at work in the library, it sometimes came back at night, when she was alone in her room. Her windows faced west, she listened to a small radio as the sun set behind the trees, igniting them and the distant horizon in its red and orange glow before the purple hand of dusk slowly took hold and night descended over the house and the woods around it. If all was quiet, if no voices penetrated the thin evening air, she left her room and walked across the lawns, down through the woods to the banks of the river. She found some comfort there, at dusk the guardians of the river changed hands, and the swans and mallards of the day were replaced by bats darting in and around the trees overhanging the banks. For a while they were her only company, then in the darkness of night they disappeared and the woodland echoed with the call of owls. If she moved to walk, the pigeons roosting above her scattered. She heard rustlings in the leaves and brambles beside the path, a path that had no doubt been walked by Victorian ladies in elegant gowns many years before her. They too would have had their share of sorrow. The house, however, was altogether a different matter, she felt unwelcome, as if it did not want her. Did the other inhabitants feel the same, was that why they never spent any time there?

The new farming methods had changed the landscape from close hedgerows and small fields to one of rolling hills that seemed to rise up and almost touch the blue horizon. Now, apart from the grunting of the machines, the fields were silent. There were no rustlings in the hedge, no larks overhead, and yet she had remembered things differently. She remembered staring up at the hawthorn and brambles edged by nettles to the sky above, clasping her mother's hand as they walked between the fields to the village shop. Her mother used to tell her which bird was a thrush, a hedge sparrow, or a blackbird, and point out the skylarks high overhead.

She decided to retrace her steps across the fields instead of fighting through the nettles and brambles that led her to the woodland of Bodding Dean. Soon the sun would set, and she made for her room as the other creatures scurried for their nests and shelter. As night fell she would sit and listen to the radio and read, complete in her solitude. Her only contact with the outside world was at the library and everyone who worked there had a wife or husband, children and pets, and their talk was of schools, their families, and their next holiday. It underlined her loneliness.

* * *

Hermione

'Have you got anything on Bonsai?' It was a Wednesday morning, she had been checking the shelves in the biography section for *Eastern Approaches* by Fitzroy McClain, the hardback had become sought after and it seemed that someone had taken a fancy to the library's copy.

'I'm sorry?'

'Bonsai, you know, little trees in little trays!'

The voice was warm but strong; its speaker stood a good twelve inches above her and looked down onto her. He had dark brown eyes and black hair that fell lazily across his forehead almost to his shoulders, which were broad and covered by a paint stained T-shirt. He was suntanned and smiling at her.

'It would be in the gardening section, over there', she pointed in the direction behind him.

'Thanks.' He turned towards the back of the library, illuminated as he walked by the shafts of sunlight which shone like torch beams through the small dark windows of the old building. Hermione found Eastern Approaches, it was tucked behind a copy of Anne Frank's Diary. She had read all the biographies on the shelves, many of them whilst she was still up north, alone in the quiet of another room, in another time.

She went back to the desk and updated the database to reflect one hard copy of *Eastern Approaches*.

She was glad it had not been stolen. Not really a woman's book she mused, but then perhaps men should read *Wuthering Heights* or *The Tenant of Wildfell Hall*. Especially *The Tenant of Wildfell Hall* she thought.

'Can I take this then please?' He was back, stooping slightly this time so that they seemed altogether closer. As he held the book out, she noticed that his hand and arm were badly scarred, as if the skin had melted and reformed. The scar continued up his arm to the edge of a black tattoo, the rest of which was concealed beneath the sleeve of his T-shirt. He was smiling, the book he held was *Eastern Approaches*. 'You haven't got anything on Bonsai, I saw you looking at this so I thought I'd give it a go. What's it like, have you read it?'

'It's really good, it starts with a journey to Samarkand and Bokhara,' she blushed slightly, wondering how he got the scars. He opened the book which revealed the exotic face and enigmatic smile of the author, and the quote from Flecker 'For lust of knowing what should not be known we take the golden road to Samarkand'. She noticed that his other hand and arm were scarred equally badly, although slightly differently, but like the other arm the scar ran all the way to the sleeve of his T-shirt beneath which was another black tattoo.

'Well', he smiled, 'I'll give it a go, here's my card',

and he handed it over.

'Matthew Doyle?' she said unnecessarily, perhaps to cover the silence whilst she typed his name into the database, perhaps to divert any attention to the awful scarring on the hands which held the card. She looked up and smiled 'I hope you like it' and blushed again slightly, feeling self-conscious. His smile broke her uneasiness.

'Thanks, if you're around when I bring it back I'll let you know!' He was still smiling, and he turned and walked out through the doors into the dazzling sunlight.

The heat built up throughout the day. Behind the main door of the library two glass internal doors remained closed, and not a breath of air rustled the daily newspapers or the leaves on the solitary aspidistra which stood in a white pot at the end of the desk. She was glad when the working day drew to a close, the computers were switched off and she was able to tidy up, putting away reference books left out, the newspapers, the thick-paged children's books which lay scattered on the floor at the far end. She stooped down to collect her bag from beneath the desk and as she straightened herself she was confronted yet again by the large muscular frame of Matthew Doyle. Taken by surprise, she gasped audibly.

'I know! Twice in one day is a bit much, but I decided to skive off, it was such a beautiful day and I

have a lust of knowing what should not be known!'
He was smiling again, and she couldn't help but
warm to him, she felt her face reddening again.

'Oh I didn't mean to ... well ... you know ... I
was surprised, we're closing up now and I didn't
expect anybody to come in.'

'Well you see, I've done nothing but read all day.
Once I started, I couldn't put it down and when I fin-
ished I thought I'd drop it in and say thank you.
Thanks!'

The book was common ground and she felt more
comfortable. She remembered how McClean had
seduced her with the description of his initial journey across the Caspian to Central Asia.

'Actually, I liked the book so much I'm going to
buy a copy' he said.

'Oh, I think it's out of print, I'm pretty sure the
hardback is but sometimes they reprint them in
paperback. Come to think of it I think it has been
reprinted in paperback. I could check for you if you
want me to?' It was probably the longest sentence
she had spoken for a month.

'Thanks, thanks a lot, I should do that myself
though shouldn't I? I don't want to be a pain. Anyway,
I'm sorry to come in when you're obviously closing
... uh ... I was on my way for a beer, do you wanna
come along?'

She was still grasping the book. The golden road to

Samarkand? she said, surprising herself again.

'If you want. It's the pub round the corner.'

Something prevented her from saying 'I don't drink', something blocked out the smell of beer on her father's breath, and she heard herself saying 'Okay then. I've shut down here, I've just got to do the lights and the alarm and lock up.'

They walked out into the evening sun through the narrow streets to a small cobbled square with a church on one side and a pub on the other.

It was dimly lit, the prevailing smell that of beer, cigarette smoke hung in the air. Matthew nodded at one or two people sitting drinking, his large form stooping beneath the oak beams in the ceiling. 'Evening Matthew. What's it to be then?' The publican was chubby, dark haired, with a beard and brown eyes that darted onto Hermione and back again to Matthew before she had time to register the smile on his face. Matthew turned to her. 'What would you like?'

'I don't usually drink.' She tried not to sound cold, but the smell of the beer had taken her back to the kitchen at home; the bloated redness of the publican's face to that of her father's. She felt foolish. Matthew diverted the publican.

'I'll have a pint please Lloyd' he said.

'Usual?'

'Yeah, that'll be fine', he said and turned back to

Hermione. 'Have a glass of white wine or some-thing', he suggested.

She had recovered slightly. 'Okay then!' It wasn't beer and it wasn't whisky and she wasn't going to become like her father. They went outside and sat beneath a large umbrella, a beech tree and the blue sky above it.

'A car crash' said Matthew.

'I'm sorry?' she said.

'You want to know about the scars. They're burns, from a car crash three or four years ago. I was the lucky one!' he smiled.

'Oh, I wasn't, I mean …'

'It's all right. I'd rather get that one out of the way. And yes, I have got some on the rest of my body, and yeah, I am a bit hung up about them still, but then again, they're a good talking point!'

'What about the tattoos then? They're not from a car crash are they?' she smiled, surprising herself.

He laughed. 'No, I got them done when I was six-teen, when I got my first bike, we all did … me and my mates … probably not such a good idea now. Anyway, that's my life story, what about yours?'

She had finished her wine, and before she could answer, Matthew was up and on his way to the bar, smiling at her. He came back with more beer and a large glass of chilled white wine. She liked it.

'Where are you from then?' he asked.

'Near Blackburn. I was born near here but my Mum and Dad moved up there when I was young'.

They chatted. He told her more about his accident, his time in hospital afterwards, what it was like growing up in the countryside she had left behind.

'We went a bit wild really, some of my mates still live out in the woods, they've become travellers, work in the summer, go off all winter.'

He was working as a painter and decorator, the organiser of several of them who worked together on different jobs, locally or sometimes up in London. She bought him another drink and had another large glass of wine herself, it dulled some senses and enlivened others. The sun was still warm, shadows grew longer and the other tables outside were slowly taken up.

'I'd better get going' said Matthew, 'd'you want a lift anywhere?' She hesitated. 'I've got to go and price a job' he said, sensing her caution.

'Okay then, I live up at Bodding Dean Hall, do you know it, it's the big old house along April Lane towards Dulverton.'

'Yeah, no problem, I ride past it a lot – let's go! It's starting to fill up here anyway.'

They walked back out into the square, he led her past the church, down a small lane. 'I've parked just along here' he said, 'near the duck pond.' They arrived in a small empty car park except for a large motorcycle standing in one corner with two chrome exhausts either side, and a green and cream fuel tank. It had Triumph written clearly on it. The chrome reflected the golden rays of the evening sun. 'It's a bit of a dinosaur really, but I like it and ride it around in the summer. I've got another bike that I use quite a bit, but this one's my favourite.'

'It's beautiful! What is it?'

Matthew smiled. 'It's a T120 Bonneville, a lot slower than it looks!' The bike was immaculate, its symmetrical beauty self evident. Matthew unlocked the heavy chain between the wheel and forks, and handed Hermione one of the two helmets which it also secured. 'You've gotta put one of these on' he said. 'You haven't been on a bike before have you?'

'No. Never had the chance, that's all' she answered defiantly.

He took the bike off the stand, turned the key, kick-started it into life, at the same time got on and steadied it so that she could get on the pillion.

'Hold on! Stick your arms around my waist and lean with me when we go round corners. That's all you need to do other than enjoy yourself!' She had to lift her skirt really high above her knees to be able to sit across the pillion, and the noise of the bike and the full length of her legs as they drove through the small town caused a few looks.

Then they were out on the open road, the sun

warmed her back and everything changed as Matthew opened up the throttle on a long straight bordered by fields of maize. There were no other vehicles on the road, she knew they were going fast but felt safe. Adrenaline was pumping round her body and she was excited, the wind rushed over her, she held him tightly and for a while the world was theirs.

April Lane was small and narrow, they slowed and approached the house from the west as the lane rose beneath the shadow of trees that grew out of the banks on either side, their roots washed by the rain so that they stood proud of the bank, twisted and knarled. A pheasant hesitated in front of them, Matthew stopped to let it by and then they swept up the drive to the entrance of Bodding Dean Hall.

'Nice place' said Matthew swinging off the Boneville, and holding it whilst Hermione did the same.

'That was fantastic!' she blurted, pulling her skirt down.

'Yeah, probably felt fast to you did it? Anyway, I'm glad you liked it. I've gotta get going now, go and price this job. I need some books on gardening so maybe I'll see you in the library sometime.'

He seemed very slightly distant, she was so elevated and he should have been the same. He sensed her slight disappointment, 'I don't wanna go and price this job but I've got to.' He smiled. She was reassured.

She went up the stairs to her room and watched the sun sink behind the trees, it warmed her, and she opened the window to hear a blackbird singing from the yew tree below.

Chapter

4

IT WAS SATURDAY AND SHE HAD TO WORK. THE HOT weather had continued, the council insisted that the glass doors remained shut so that by midday the heat was overbearing. It was quiet, the building was empty except for herself. She wouldn't be able to go out for lunch, there was no one to cover her break and she was resigned to another five and half hours of heat and solitude. She had tidied up, the children's books were neatly arranged ready to be mauled again on Monday morning by toddlers before they went to the crèche in the building next door. She took down the copy of *Eastern Approaches* and began to re-read the opening pages, pausing at one of her favourite paragraphs. It told the story of a Persian architect who had built the Bibi Kahanum, of how he had fallen in love with a Princess and kissed her so passionately on the cheek that it had left a burn. When the Persian ruler saw this he sent his men to kill the architect but he fled from them and got to the top of the highest minaret. Then, as he was about to be seized by his pursuers, he sprouted wings and soared high above Samarkand.

The glass partition doors opened and a shadow cast itself on the main desk, where she sat reading. She knew it was Matthew and she smiled as she looked up.

'Hello.'

'Hi. How are you?'

'Oh, I'm fine, rushed off my feet as you can see!'

'I bought you some drinks – I don't know what you like so there's some different ones. OJ, Coke, water – I didn't think you'd want any beer if you're working.'

'That's brilliant, thanks! I don't like beer, my dad's an alcoholic and he used to drink loads of it so it sort of put me off.'

'Yeah, I can see that. Wine's still alright though is it?' he smiled.

'Yes. thanks.' She smiled back.

'Er, some mates of mine are doing a gig tonight.

Hermione

It's in a pub about four or five miles away, it's a nice place and I wondered if you might wanna come along?'

'Alright, why not?! What sort of music is it?'

'I dunno really. They're all travellers, they've got acoustic guitars, violins, a drummer, an electric guitar, it's a right mixture but they're really good. I'll take you out there anyway, if that's alright, I mean, there are no buses so you'd have to get a lift anyway.'

'On your bike?'

'Yeah, I'll pick you up straight from here if you want, about six, that's when you finish isn't it?'

'Okay, but I'd quite like to change and sort myself out a bit. I'll meet you somewhere, at that pub or something?'

'I could pick you up in April Lane, it's only five minutes away. They go on about nine o'clock so we'd still have plenty of time to get there, have a drink or two before they go on. Does that sound okay?'

'Yeah, I'll see you then! Thanks.' She smiled as the glass doors opened and a youngish woman in her 30's came in with two young children. 'My other customers!' Hermione half whispered, laughing. 'See you tonight!'

Matt smiled, and reached to hold the door open for the woman who was struggling with shopping as well as the children.

At eight o'clock the sun was still high in the sky, it

hovered like a large orange disk above the Downs. She held tight to Matt as he weaved through the lanes towards it, as if it were a beacon and the summer solstice had not yet passed. She could see sheep in the distance grazing on the slopes of the hills; the air was warm and alive, and like before it flowed over her, caressing, penetrating.

The pub stood alone in a small valley. To either side of it was post and rail fencing, water troughs and sheep pens where several people were walking with scruffy dogs. Others were hanging around outside the pub, swilling beer, smoking, leaning on bikes, laughing and joking. Quite a few were tattooed and a lot of bodies were pierced in various places. More dogs scampered around, in and out of the bikes and their owners, chased by toddlers and older children who were having water fights. Matt pulled up, swung off the bike first and held it unobtrusively for Hermione as she got down from the pillion. He had taken his helmet off and was saying hello to some of the people outside, and introduced Hermione to them, calling her H. She smiled and said hello and then they went inside to the bar, opposite the small stage, an un-miked drum kit, Marshall stacks and a small PA with three black triangular speaker cabinets set down for the foldback. The pub was heaving, and there was a distinct smell of black hash in the air. Matt smiled. 'Some of these people aren't very discreet. We can smoke a joint outside if you want?' He looked at her and then he said 'Sorry. You don't smoke do you?'

'No – never really came across it all that much, you know, I was looking after my dad and … well … I never went out much and I just lived in my own world there really.'

'Best way' he said. 'For this lot it's a way of life. It can become a real habit, never mind what it does to your lungs!'

'Why do you smoke it then?' she asked.

'Habit!' he laughed and she laughed with him. 'Would you like another glass of wine? What's it like, is it any good?'

'Yeah, thanks, it's really nice, I think I've found my drug!'

The band came on stage and looked extraordinary. The line-up seemed to be bass, drums, guitar, keyboards, a female violinist, three female back-up singers and a male vocalist. They were well rehearsed and well sound checked, and without much ado went straight into their first number. The quality of their musicianship was apparent from the first ten seconds, reminiscent of the Pogues at their best. Within about thirty seconds half the audience was on its feet. Matt and Hermione sat at the back and she was over-awed as the band weaved its magic. There was a brief pause in between the first and second number, allowing her to shout 'they're brilliant!' and squeeze Matt's hand in appreciation. He nodded his head and grinned.

'They play a very long set!' Matt shouted in her ear after half an hour or so. 'Do you fancy some fresh air?' She nodded yes and they left the pub and went outside into the fields with the water troughs and sheep enclosures. Some of the children were still running around, one or two parents were there too, smoking very long cigarettes.

'I'm old fashioned' said Matt. 'I don't think people should smoke dope round their kids, 'til its legal anyway!'

'Have you got any?' asked Hermione.

'Dope or kids?'

'Dope!'

'Uh, yeah. Why?'

'Well, it's about time I tried some isn't it?' she said.

'Well, it's up to you. There's a good and bad side to dope, too much makes you lazy and forgetful, and smoking is bad for you. There, that's your health warning! Do you still want some?'

'Yes! I feel like I missed out, all those years .... Well ...'

They sat down next to one of the sheep enclosures on an old tree trunk facing the hills.

'As good a place as any' said Matt as he pulled out

HERMIONE

a cigarette tin and opened it to get out the skins, tobacco and hash inside. 'I've got some grass too, it's home grown, the hydroponic stuff, it's really good, would you rather have that?'

'Okay then, let's smoke that. Maybe there's no need to put any tobacco in it then?'

And so he rolled a two skinner of a Northern Lights female plant he'd harvested the day before. He took two or three large tokes, held the smoke in his lungs and passed the joint to Hermione who copied him and handed it back. They did this a few more times until they finished it. Matt smiled. 'Would you like another glass of wine? It'll be easy to get to the bar because everyone will be up dancing and down the front by now. I wouldn't mind another beer, it's that sort of night!'

'I'd love some wine, thanks.'

The sun was sinking, she sat and watched the light change, one perfect moment becoming another. One of the dogs came up to her wagging his tail, his cunning eyes beguiling. She stroked his head, scratched him gently behind his ears and he was delighted. He looked slyly at some rabbits in a distant corner of the field, but her soothing hand persuaded him to roll over on his back, allowing her to stroke him and gently scratch his chest. She gazed back towards the sun as it was finally eclipsed by the hills, crowning them with fire as it sank behind them. The air was heavy with wild honeysuckle entwined in the hedge where she sat, and its scent became intoxicating, all prevailing. The dog got up and scampered off towards the car park where Matt was leaving the pub with their drinks.

'Hi! How are you doing?'

'Fine! I made a friend.' She smiled.

'Yeah, that's Zipper, Charlie's dog. He found him when he was a pup in a zipped up jacket dumped at the bus stop.'

'I wouldn't mind finding a dog like him!' she smiled.

'Yeah, he's alright isn't he. Do you wanna sit here for a while or would you like to go back in and check out the band again?'

'It's nice here. Shall we have a drink and then go back in?'

'Yeah, why not!' he said and sat down next to her, handing her the glass of wine.

'Hmmm! Tastes like I'm drinking this honeysuckle!' she said, giggling.

'Beautiful smell isn't it? I love it'. He seemed warm and confident, at ease with his surroundings, with nature. Something about him was unusually strong; trust perhaps, she might be able to trust him. They sat in the field, surrounded by the fullness of the summer evening as night descended on the valley.

'The band will be finishing soon, shall we go back

HERMIONE

in and catch the last few numbers?' Matt asked.

'Yes, why not! It is beautiful here though isn't it?!' she said.

'Yeah. How do you find the grass, are you okay?'

'Yeah, I feel really good, let's go!'

They stayed and watched the end of the band's set for about twenty minutes, various encores, and then spilled out with the rest of the audience back into the coolness of the night.

'Some people are gonna go on now, but I reckon there'll be a lock-in later on' said Matt. 'Do you want to wait around or shall we go?'

'We could go back to Bodding Dean. There's a place near there we could go for a while if you like' she suggested.

'Okay, let's do that.'

A few minutes later she was clinging on tight to him again as they rode back over the hills towards the village. The moon had come up, it was almost full, lighting up the fields and hedgerows as they swept past her, until they reached the drive of Bodding Dean. Matt slowed the bike and swung carefully up into the long drive.

'Where's this place then?' he said.

She laughed. 'Ah, it's this way, come on!'

She grabbed his hand and led him through the full-scented rose beds across the lawns, down through the woods to the river which ran like mercury beneath the moon. She led him to her favourite spot, under the large maple tree set just back from the water. They were quiet. Bats swooped out from the oak near the bank and darted across the silver water to scoop up insects which still hovered there, then back round again flying close over their heads. Matt raised his eyebrows and smiled. He put his arm round her and pulled her closer to him, she responded, turned her head and their mouths met eagerly. It was a long kiss, passionate and knowing, tender and loving. They broke off.

'Wow!' she said, 'you've done that before haven't you!'

'It takes two you know!' he smiled, then she pulled him towards her.

'Let's go back' she whispered. 'Back up to the house.' She held his hand tightly and stood up, pulling him with her, to pick their way through the nettles and brambles up to the lawns, the rose beds and her room.

'I haven't got anything to drink' she said, 'I'm sorry.'

'That's alright' he said smiling, stepping forward to clasp her round the waist. She leaned her head back to look up at him, they kissed again, deeply. She slid her hands inside his T-shirt up his back and pulled him hard towards her. The bed was the main piece of furniture in the room, he turned and guided her onto it, kissing her mouth, her hair, her neck. Warmth, strength and passion invaded her, she took off her dress, and helped him off with his jeans and T-shirt.

Making love for them was natural, yet passionate, enduring and disturbing. There was recognition, they fitted together like a puzzle, it was profound, almost shocking that it could be so perfect. It was that perhaps which disturbed. The curtains were open and the moon probed her room. They drank orange juice, gazed quietly at each other, and made love and slept and made love.

Dawn broke with the blackbird's song from the yew tree outside the open window. She made tea and they ate some chocolate, a bar she had forgotten about, that lay uneaten in a coat pocket.

Chapter

5

OVER THE NEXT MONTH THEY SAW EACH OTHER whenever they could. They were both working during the day, but in the evening they went out. They had their favourite places, the pub up on the Downs, their spot by the river. He took her to his place in town, but most nights were spent at Bodding Dean in her room. They lay on the bed as the amber light of the setting sun played on the walls and the ceilings, illuminating the elaborate Victorian cornice, the plaster ceiling rose of wild fruit and ivy. It flickered on the dark oak floorboards, on the old fireplace like the one her mother had at home.

'Do you ever feel you were born in the wrong time?' he said as they lay on her bed.

'I don't know ... sometimes I feel we've met before. I can relax with you, I can't relax around other people, I don't feel that I fit in.'

'Yeah, I know what you mean.'

'I thought you liked other people.'

'Some people, some times.'

'I mean, usually you seem pretty relaxed, you know, with your mates and in the pub.'

'I get by, I'm a loner really, like you!' and he pulled her close to him and kissed her gently, but she broke off, insistent.

'Why though?' she asked, stroking his forehead, running her fingers through his hair.

'I don't know. I think the world we live in has cut us off from our real selves. For ages I thought it was just me, but now I don't know, I'm beginning to think there's more to it, you know ... there's no trust is there? You can't trust the government, they just manage the people for themselves. If you look at all the technology that's available now it's not that difficult for them to do. You've read a lot of books, Orwell was right in a lot of ways ... maybe we should join my mates in their vans, just live in the woods.'

'My dad used to talk a bit like you sometimes, you know, about control, he called it 'they'. He said that governments didn't really govern, behind them was a whole load of other people who had the control, the real power. He never spoke about it that much though, he just got drunk.'

'Can't say I blame him really!' They lazed on the bed and slowly drifted into making love as the evening descended, as they lay together on the edge of darkness.

* * *

The weeks passed, slowly the evenings began to draw in, and there was a slight chill in the air. Cobwebs glistened with moisture in the early morning sun, the blackberries came and went, and the children went back to school, their bags heavily laden.

'It will be time to put the Bonnie away soon' Matt said. 'It's a bit sad but it takes too much looking after in the winter.' The decorating business slowed down for him then, and he helped his uncle restoring antiques and occasionally repairing clocks in a shop in town.

'I've always liked it' he said 'old clocks, time, how we use it, how we see it, I even tried to read that book by Hawking, you know.'

'What did it say?'

'Ah, stuff about black holes and Einstein and something about there may be even more black holes than the number of visible stars. I suppose the point is we are a very small part of something very big.'

She liked how he was open about what he thought, unlike Philip or her father even, who both had a way of hiding their inner most secrets. She was happy with Matt, and she realized that she had fallen in love with him.

They both got up early, Matt began work at 8 o'clock and was always up at the crack of dawn. Sometimes they'd been awake anyway, lying together, touching, perhaps making love or talking. She was never tired, she had endless energy, they both did.

'You've hardly had any sleep again! ' she said.

'The power of love!' he grinned, as he was getting dressed, and walked over to put the kettle on.

She lay in bed for half an hour or so, and then got up, had a bath, dressed and walked for twenty minutes or so into town to the library. Sometimes she passed the post van on its way up to the house, never minding that there would be no mail for her. As she went downstairs on this morning, she felt, for no particular reason, there might be a letter for her. She gave it no further thought, passed the van as usual on her way down the drive and made her way to work.

In the evening, as she walked up the large stone steps of the porch into the main hall of the house, she noticed a letter addressed to her lying on the top of the old piano where letters often remained un-opened for days or weeks, addressed to previous occupants who had long since disappeared.

The post mark was from Preston, and inside was a brief note from Mrs Moore. Her father had pneumonia and had been taken into hospital. He was gravely ill. She felt fear and guilt, her heart beat quickly, her face flushed. She must go, go before it was too late. She ran up the stairs to her room, some of Matthew's clothes lay scattered on the bed next to her own but it would be more than an hour or so before he came back. She had to go now, there was no time to do anything other than pack, leave him a note and make her way to the station.

She was going to make the journey home she thought she would never make. Back to the quiet dark of their old house, to the stale smell of beer and whisky. She had never been able to remove her father's presence from the depths of herself. Sometimes, as she sat alone in her room, his voice would enter her thoughts, haphazardly, if for example she was thinking about Matt. She would imagine her father saying 'you don't think that pratt'll stay with you do you?! He'll soon be off with another lass, you're too plain for the likes of him.'

It began to rain. At first a few drops appeared like pin pricks on the glass of the railway carriage window, glistening in the thin light. Then it grew heavier, blurring her vision as she looked out of the window. She felt uneasy, uneasy leaving Matt, fearful that something would go wrong. Life was fragile after all. Did we just drift in and out of each others lives, could we direct the outcome, or were we guided by other elements? She had sworn never to go back, yet here she was. With Matthew she lived in a world cut off from the past, in a kind of eternal present. Now she felt shackled, smothered by the grip of what had gone before. How long would all this take, if he was an invalid how could she leave him on his own, with no-one to care for him?

The train hurtled past the fields which nestled in the lea of the distant hills. Then the grass began to be replaced by buildings, industrial sheds and houses squashed in along the banks of the railway line. She had crossed London in a daze, and the electric hub of Euston was replaced by countryside. Other passengers got on and off, she avoided any eye contact, any hint of possible conversation. She half opened her eyes to the seat opposite where an old man sat gazing out of the window onto the rain that still fell. Soon they would reach the aqueduct and the river on the out-skirts of town, and she would be able to see the old mills and factories near the school.

It was dark and the rain had slowed to a drizzle when she got out at Preston and took a taxi straight to the hospital. It was outside of visiting hours but they were going to let her see him anyway, and it added to her unease. She made her way down the long corridors of yellow paint, stone floors, an all-pervading smell of disinfectant, until she arrived at one of the men's wards which her father shared with three others. His bed was at the end, screened off, and he was lying on his back. To his side was a metal frame containing a small glass bottle, an IV drip going into his left arm. A clear plastic tube came out of his mouth, his flesh had no substance. Tears welled in her eyes as she stood beside him, listening to him breathe, gurgling, as if he was breathing through water. It was an ominous, rattling sound. A nurse approached her, and she turned. 'Is he in pain?' she asked.

'You can see for yourself' she replied.

Hermione looked at her, confused, hurting. Was he or wasn't he? 'Is he in pain or not?!'

'He's on a diamorphine drip. He can't feel that much …'

Hermione went to the bed and held his hand. It was cold, and she gasped audibly. 'It's the circulation … that's why' the nurse said.

'How long? … How long has he got?'

'We don't know. It could be today, tomorrow, in the night. It's not long, he should be in on his own somewhere, but we've got no room.' The nurse walked off, down through the ward to the large corridor. Hermione sat on his bed, clasped his hand and wept.

'Dad! Dad! It's me, can you hear me?' But there

was only the gurgling from his lungs, he didn't stir.

After sometime, she had no idea how long, the nurse came back and felt his pulse. Her eyes met with Hermione's. 'He's gone hasn't he.'

'Yes, I'm so sorry.' The nurse came over and put her hand on Hermione's shoulder, she sobbed uncontrollably.

'I need to get a doctor love, you know … you just stay for a minute, she's just in the other ward.'

The doctor seemed about the same age as Hermione, she could barely have been five years older.

'It's a relief,' she said. 'You're his daughter aren't you, his only one?'

'Yes. I didn't know he was ill until it was too late!' she sobbed.

'There was nothing you could have done, don't blame yourself. Would you like to stay here for a little while or have you got somewhere to go?'

The doctor was from the south, her voice shared the clipped precision with some of the women in the library. She was meaning to be kind but to Hermione it sounded cold. She would go to Mrs Moore.

'I've got somewhere to go.' She left Mrs Moore's address and telephone number with them, then made her way back along the corridors and stepped out into the night to look for a taxi.

Chapter

6

SHE FUMBLED IN HER BAG FOR KEYS TO THE FRONT DOOR. It was pitch black, but she remembered well enough how to find the lock in the dark. She felt for the light switch in the hallway, it lit the stairs in front of her and the deep well of memories the house contained. It shone on the fireplace in the living room through the half open door, on the chair where he would sit having his supper, on the photograph of her mother which gazed at her. She made her way to the kitchen, and it was as if he had just left. His empty plate sat on the table, egg-stained, a bottle of brown sauce beside it. There was his mug of tea half finished, a side plate graced by a piece of toast from which a bite had been taken. Her mother's fruit bowl stood defiantly in the middle of the table, inside it a brown withered apple was surrounded by some envelopes of about the same colour – government style ones, lucky to have made it beyond the fire in the living room. She went to the pantry. It was full of beer cans, some empty lying on the floor and some full, still on the shelves next to a whisky bottle. She picked it up, went back to the kitchen, found a clean mug and poured herself a large measure. She gulped it down, poured another and took it with her as she made her way back to the hallway to go up the stairs.

His bed was unmade, pyjamas were scattered on the floor next to his work clothes. There were more beer cans in his bedroom, tossed around on the floor, one stood on the bedside table. Next to it was a photograph of her and her mother, it must have been taken around the time he used to come home from work and push her shrieking up to the sky on her swing, when those big hands held only glasses of tea or lemonade, when they picked her up and held her close to him and she felt safe and warm.

She sat on the bed and sobbed. She drank the whisky down in one gulp, but it didn't stop the sobbing. She got up, collected his pyjamas from the floor, folded them and made his bed. Then she picked up his work clothes and put them back on the chair where they used to be. He would say to her 'Look, see, I can find anything in the dark, I can! If ought should happen, I always like to know where me boots are!'

She remembered she used to dream as a child that she sat at the top of the stairs and listen to him below, in the hallway, talking on the telephone. Something came out of her room, she couldn't see it, it was like a ghost and it covered her with a sheet. Through it she could still see her father and she shouted, terrified, calling 'Daddy! Daddy!', but he couldn't hear her and he carried on talking. Then she would wake up.

She went downstairs to the kitchen, and the whisky. She had a re-fill, and went back up the stairs. She would sleep in his room, hoping desperately his spirit would come back to the house, he would know she was there waiting for him, waiting to say goodbye. She lay down on his bed, gulped some more whisky and slid into an uneasy sleep.

She woke, staring towards the foot of the bed, to where she thought he might be, but there was no-one, there was nothing. She drifted back into sleep again until the pale winter light traced its way slowly into the room, and she woke again. She went to the bathroom and washed in cold water, dried herself with his towel before going downstairs to the kitchen to make some tea. Although it was early, she would go and see Mrs Moore.

She walked down the street to the echo of a little girl's voice from a swing, 'Daddy! Higher, push me higher!'

She soon passed the sweet shop and reached Mrs Moore's house who opened the door before Hermione could ring the bell.

'I was up early, I can never sleep these days! I saw you coming down the street, just like you used to when you were a little girl!' She was tearful, holding open her arms and Hermione fell into them. 'I'm so sorry!' said Mrs Moore. 'He just got the flu, one day he was alright, then he went down with it and suddenly it was pneumonia.

They sat in her kitchen, around a large brown teapot. 'You'll have to bury him my love – I'll help with all that, the arrangements. I know, I've done it all before, I did it for my Harry, God rest his soul!'

When she left Mrs Moore, she walked past the house to the park. The morning traffic was beginning with buses into town, and one or two schoolchildren were huddled in the bus shelter. The screech of a distant train cracked the air. If only she'd seen him once more before he died, to say goodbye. The park reminded her of Philip and she soon left, back to the house, to the memories that lay there waiting for her.

This time, instead of going to her father's room,

she went down the corridor, to the room at the end which was once hers. From the window she could see the treetops in the park, now stripped of their leaves, and they waved their skeletal greeting as they moved to and fro in the wind. She was a little girl again; she had been off school with a bad cold and had got out of bed to stare out of the window. Her mother scolded her, 'Hermione, you're to stay in bed, how many times must you be told!' And she tucked her up beneath the duvet with a hot water bottle. When her father came home from work he came straight up to see her, he'd always bring her a bar of chocolate when she was ill. 'How's my little girl?! 'Ere y' are, lass, this'll make you feel better! Don't tell your mother and make sure you eat all your tea or she'll know, and she'll be after me!'

One day she did tell her mother, who only smiled. 'You're both daft! As if I didn't know!'

Her room was almost untouched. He must have been in there, he'd put some of her dolls out that she'd long ago put away, and they stared at her now from the top of her chest of drawers, in mute sympathy. He'd also replaced one of the pictures on the wall, a modern print, with a scene of a picnic by woodland creatures.

She had had to grow up fast when her mother died and he lost his wife and little girl almost together. Each day beneath the grey metal sky on his way to work he must have searched for a reason to go on, to walk through the works gate. Perhaps she hadn't been enough, herself heartbroken at her mother's death, trying to cope, and now it was too late.

The door bell rang. Her heart skipped a beat, for the split second that it rung she was suspended in time, in the world of the child. It was Mrs Moore.

'Just thought I'd pop in love, to see how you're doing.'

'Oh, I'm fine. Thanks. Come in. It's a bit of a mess I'm afraid, I haven't had time to tidy up or anything ...'

'That's alright Hermione, I'll give you a hand. He was never a great one for tidying was he?'

They went in the kitchen, washed up the plates and tidied.

'When my Harry went, I never thought I'd get over it, but you do you know. It takes a long time, and they're always with you, somewhere. You sit down here now, we'll have a brew, I've been in touch about the arrangements, it's all sorted out so there's nothing you need to worry about.' The funeral was set for two days time.

'I thought the sooner the better' said Mrs Moore.

'Thanks' said Hermione. 'I don't know what I'd do without you' she smiled.

'Ah! You've always been my favourite, such a bonnie wee thing!'

HERMIONE

Outside it was raining again, winter was closing its grip and the cold and damp were penetrating. Mrs Moore persuaded Hermione to go back with her, to her house, to bath and get some rest. She was grateful for the respite from the memories, from the ghosts which waylaid her at every turn.

* * *

For the next two days Mrs Moore helped her to go through her father's things and put them neatly into boxes. They sent the best clothes to the charity shop, and threw away the pyjamas, work clothes and things that no-one else would want. They cleaned the house, got rid of the beer cans and empty whisky bottles, scrubbed the floors, and set up a table in the living room for tea after the funeral.

'There'll be some of his drinking mates there love, you'd best prepare yourself. They'll not be wanting a brew, we'd better have something stronger!' said Mrs Moore, and they went out to the off-licence on the corner to get whisky and beer.

'He was still well-liked you know, a lot of them will be here just for the drink won't they, but that mustn't upset you. He wouldn't begrudge them that!'

The day of the funeral came, heralded by a grey sky and the hiss of traffic going into town in the early morning. Hermione spent the night in his room again, sleeping fitfully, but no ghost came to visit her, no spirit comforted her with the glimpse of an after-life. She slept with the sound of silence.

Mrs Moore, true to her word, had indeed seen to everything. She had arranged to come round to the house at around 10.30am to make sure that they would be ready for 'afterwards'. Her father's mates, having found out his fate, were determined to give him a good send-off.

The doorbell rang just after 10.30am and she let Mrs Moore inside, laden with parcels of food, home-baked cakes, scones, some sandwiches and more whisky.

'That's eight cases of beer and four bottles of whisky now!' said Hermione. 'And look at all the food! Surely nobody's going to eat that are they?!'

'You'd be surprised love. When my Harry went we had to send out for more, from chippy up road in the end! Don't take this the wrong way now, but nothing gives you an appetite like a good funeral! Ah! Come 'ere now, c'mon, give Mrs M a cuddle!'

She held her arms open. 'There, there! You'll be alright, we musn't let him down now. He'll be watching you see, he'll want to know everyone has a good time!'

'Do you think so? Do you think he'll be watching … Do you believe in … in?'

HERMIONE

'In God and all that?' said Mrs Moore.

'Well in anything, you know, any sort of life after death?'

'Oh, I don't know my dear. I swear I saw Harry once, as plain as could be walking up the garden path! But I don't know, perhaps it's all in the mind. The important thing is that you know you loved him, and well … the drink … there was nothing you could do, not after your Mum went, not really.'

'But he seemed to change even before then' said Hermione. 'I remember he stopped coming home early, he stopped playing with me. We missed him so much!'

'Ay well, a hard life you know for a man, day in day out, keeping a family. All that's supposed to have changed now, better conditions, and all this women's stuff, but I don't know, I think the women have just taken it over and it's as bad for them too, so we're all worse off! Come on now, let's have this brew and we'd best be on our way. The service is set for midday. By the time we get there and settled down … Well you know … '

The church rose up from the small newly built houses surrounding it. It seemed out of place, almost as if the houses had been there first and the church had been dropped from the sky, out of time. Yet it was defiant, its grey stone weathered and enduring, its stained glass sparkling in the thin light of the

winter sun. Gravestones surrounded it, with no particular pattern.

The churchyard was busy. Twenty or thirty people
stood outside, waiting to go in. The hearse swept
silently through the gates, Mrs Moore and Hermione
were dropped off from the following car and they
filtered in unobtrusively through the large oak doors
to the sanctuary of the church. Some taxis arrived and
dropped off others until forty or so more people were
gathered inside, none of whom she knew except Mrs
Moore. She clasped her hand, it was midday and they
stood up as the vicar began his opening sentence. It
had seemed very sudden.

'We are gathered together to remember before
God the life of Robert, Bob, whom we have known
and loved. To thank God for his life and to recall to
our minds his friendship, and to commend his soul
to the everlasting tender care of our heavenly father.
And so we pray together; 'Our father who art in
heaven, hallowed be thy name;' and the congrega-
tion stumbled through the Lord's prayer.

'Let us now sing together 'Abide With Me'.

When they had finished, he continued. 'No man is
an island, entire of itself; every man is a piece of the
continent, a part of the main ... Any man's death
diminishes me, because I am involved in mankind;
and therefore never send to know for whom the bell
tolls; it tolls for thee.'

Hermione

He continued, but it passed over Hermione. She was numb with grief. It was as if she sat alone in the church with only Mrs Moore's hand clasping hers.

Her father was buried to the rear of the church, with a committal at the graveside. One or two of his friends made comforting sounds to her, and then they began to filter off slowly, towards the front of the churchyard and the car park. The vicar came over to Hermione and Mrs Moore, smiling benignly.

'Ah! Hermione! This is so terribly upsetting for you, Mrs Moore has told me how difficult it has been these last years. What are you going to do? I expect you'll stay up for a few days will you, sort one or two things out?'

' I honestly don't know' was really all she could manage.

'Don't you worry' said Mrs Moore. 'I'll look after her, she'll be fine!'

'Well, I'll drop in and see you if that's alright during the course of the week' the vicar said, addressing Mrs Moore.

'Yes, why not! she smiled, and squeezed Hermione's hand at the same time.

'C'mon now love, we've got all the food and drink to organize!'

The vicar turned and walked back towards the church, and they followed him, treading carefully between the graves.

The sky was still heavy, full with rain, the air was damp, and Hermione shivered as the cold penetrated through her coat to the thin black lace blouse she wore underneath it. The walk back to the church was slow, as they finally approached it she could see a small crowd huddled around something or someone. The black wall of their coats and suits spread apart, and behind it was the unmistakable shape of Matthew's Boneville. It had a presence of its own, as if it too had come to say goodbye. Her heart thumped, where was he?

She got to the bike, reached out and touched it as if to make sure it was real. Nobody spoke and she stood in silence looking round. Matthew walked out of the shadows of the church, his large figure looming high above the gravestones as he passed quietly between them on his way to her. She stood by the bike and waited, her hand tightened around the handlebar.

'You forgot to leave your phone number!' He smiled. She was shivering, her hand was still fastened onto the bike. He came towards her, took hold of it, and she let go to fling her arms around him, melting into his warmth. He opened his jacket, and she put her arms around his waist. He kissed her cheeks. Nobody around them had moved, the air was heavy with silence.

Matthew spoke again. 'I brought you something,'

he smiled. There was a bag next to the rear wheel of the bike and he reached into it to pull out a heavily-lined black biker's jacket. Hermione was still shivering, and she hadn't uttered a word.

A voice from somewhere said 'You'd better try it on lass, if you stand there much longer we'll all be stiffs!'

Her dad's mates laughed and she laughed with them through her tears as she took off her coat to put on the jacket.

Matthew reached down to the bag and pulled out the helmet she used to borrow, and handed it to her. Neither of them spoke, he turned round, turned the key in the bike and kick-started it into life. Another voice from the crowd said 'Chuffing 'ell, it bloody works as well!' He got on and steadied it as she swung her legs over the pillion and grabbed his waist. Hermione looked up and saw Mrs Moore standing at the edge of the car park, and she began to walk over to them.

'Wait Matt!' said Hermione as Mrs Moore approached. 'Mrs M. this is Matt!' she said.

'Ay, and he'd best take you home! You've said goodbye to your dad, you can leave this lot to me!' she said in the same way she used to say to her when she was a little girl. 'You get on your way home now darling, there's a good lass. Don't worry, you come back up with Matt in a while, we'll all be here!' she smiled.

Matthew turned to look at her, as if silently questioning, should he stay or should he go? Mrs Moore smiled. 'Go!'

Hermione tightened her grip around his waist and squeezed. He pulled in the clutch, kicked down into first gear and they rode off. The rain that had looked so threatening stayed away, but the cold was still penetrating, even through the jacket he had bought for her. They got on the motorway almost straightaway, she felt that she was travelling through a tunnel of ice, but they kept going until Matthew pulled into the services.

He said 'You must be freezing – I am and I've got just a bit more on than you! I've brought up an old fleece that's in the bag, it should fit under your jacket.'

He rummaged around and found it for her. Food, shelter and clothing, she recalled having read somewhere were the only things that mattered. She had a faint recollection that the same person had also said that sex and love were a luxury.

'Thanks!' She shivered. 'That's much better!'

They went for a meal, lots of tea, and she began to warm up. 'I know the bottom dropped out of my world when my old man died' said Matt. 'That's supposed to be the day you become a man.'

'Why did you come up? Why did you come all the way to the churchyard?'

'Well, it's true that you forgot to leave the phone

Hermione

number and, oh, I just had to … ' He looked at her across the table of the motorway café, some children ran behind him shouting, on their way to the games arcade. 'I brought you this.' He handed her a hardback copy of *Eastern Approaches*. 'I've re-read it and decided its an early road book! It's a travellers book and, well, I don't want to travel alone anymore, I want to travel with you.'

'I suppose that'll do for now!' She smiled, reaching across the table to find his hand. He pulled her towards him, leaning forwards so their lips could meet.

An hour or so later she could see the cooling towers near Warrington in the distance, the rain that held off for so long began to fall, its predictability almost a comfort.

**TWO SURFERS IN A PARANORMAL THRILLER
SET AGAINST A BACKDROP OF REVOLUTION AND
INTRIGUE IN VIETNAM**

BASED ON A TRUE STORY BY

DANIEL TRIBE

IN EVERGREEN PAPERBACK

"I read 'FULL MOON RED SUN' straight through
from cover to cover and enjoyed it…
Daniel Tribe is clearly a writer to look out for…
and surfers will enjoy the passages set out on the waves."

FREE STATE MAGAZINE
Glastonbury

"Californian Steve plunges right into the
burgeoning hippy culture of the late 60's…
Still, the writing is pacey and entertaining, and the
surfing sequences will get you stoked."

WAVELENGTH
Europe's Premier Surfing Magazine

£5.99 plus p+p from amazon.co.uk or **£7.00** inc p+p from

EVERGREEN BOOKS
Passfield Business Centre, Lynchborough Road, Passfield,
Hampshire GU30 7SB

Tel: 01428 751 451   Fax: 01428 751 557